Larky Mavis

BROCK COLE

Larky Mavis

FARRAR STRAUS GIROUX

NEW YORK

For Charnie

Distributed in Canada by Douglas & McIntyre Ltd.
Color separations by Hong Kong Scanner Arts
Printed and bound in the United States of America by Berryville Graphics
Typography by Filomena Tuosto
First edition, 2001
1 3 5 7 9 10 8 6 4 2

Library of Congress Cataloging-in-Publication Data

Cole, Brock.

Larky Mavis / Brock Cole.— 1st ed.

p.   cm.

Summary: Having found a tiny baby in a peanut shell, Larky Mavis calls him Heart's Delight
and carries him around as he grows bigger, to the confusion and anger of the adults around her.

ISBN 0-374-34365-9

[1. Babies—Fiction.] I. Title.

PZ7.C67342 Las 2001

[E]—dc21

00-51419

Down the road came Larky Mavis, mooning about, mooning about.

"Whoops!" said Mavis, and up she went and down she came.
"Who tripped me?" she called in a brave voice.

Right in the middle of the road were three peanuts.

"A fine thing, tripping a poor girl," she said. "I'll eat you up."

The first tasted like liver and onions.

"That's good," said Mavis.

The second tasted like bread pudding.

"That's good," said Mavis, and cracked the third peanut wide open.

"Well!" she said, laughing. "I won't eat you!"

Just then the schoolmaster, out for a run with his students, popped over the hedge and into the road.

"Teacher! Teacher! Look what I got!" cried Mavis. "A little baby that I found in a peanut. I wouldn't eat him for anything."

"Gather around, Class," said the schoolmaster. "Let's see what Mavis has found. A little worm, is it? Thank you very much, Mavis, for showing us your little worm. Come, Class!"

"A worm?" Mavis watched the schoolmaster and his students flounder through the briars and up the hill.

"Well, a fine worm, then. I'll keep you in my pocket," she said, and she wrapped him up in her hankie and tucked him inside her coat.

The next Sunday after church, there was Larky Mavis, mooning about
the tombstones with an old basket over her arm.

"Now, Mavis," said the parson when he saw her. "You've been told.
You're not to hang around the church. People don't like it."

"Ah, but, Father, I want you to christen my baby."

The parson was shocked.

"Do you have a baby in that basket, Mavis? Show me at once."

Larky Mavis opened her basket. "It's a little baby that I found in a peanut. I call him Heart's Delight because he makes me glad."

"Now, Mavis," said the parson, looking in the basket, "that's a mouse you have there. You know I can't christen a mouse. Be a good girl and run along."

"A mouse?" said Mavis, running off. "Well, a sweet mouse, then."

Mavis fed Heart's Delight on the nuts and berries that she found in the hedgerows. Soon he was too big for her basket, and she carried him about on her back, wrapped in an old curtain she'd found as they went mooning about, mooning about.

One day they met the doctor in the road outside his gate.

"Doctor, Doctor," Mavis called. "Look here! My baby can't talk, and I want him to call me Ma."

The doctor looked in her bundle.

"Mavis," he said. "What you have in there isn't a baby. What you have is some kind of deformed bird or"—he looked more closely—"maybe a bat."

"Oh," said Larky Mavis. "Well, could you teach him to call me Ma?"

"No! I can't teach an animal like that to say 'Ma.' It wouldn't be natural."

Larky Mavis watched the doctor climb in his fancy car and drive away.
"Ah, well," she sighed. "Maybe you'll learn all by yourself, Heart's Delight.
What could be more natural than that?"

Heart's Delight ate and ate and grew and grew. Soon he was too big to live on nuts and berries, so Larky Mavis made soup for him from frostbitten potatoes and cabbage stalks.

He liked it very much, and what he couldn't eat, Larky Mavis gave away in the street.

People began to talk.

"What a pest that Mavis is!" said the butcher. "She's bad for business."

"And what is that thing she carries around?" asked the baker.

"It's a pig with four ears," said one person.

"A turkey in molt," said another.

"A calf and a half," said a third.

"I believe it's some kind of dragon," said the baker's wife. "It'll bite a child someday, you mark my words. Something's got to be done."

They were waiting for her the next morning when she came mooning about, mooning about.

"Now, Mavis, give us that thing you've got in your bundle," said the butcher. "We'll take care of it for you."

Mavis held on tight to Heart's Delight.

"Ah, no! You get your own baby," she cried, and off she hurried down the street.

As she passed the school, the schoolmaster was looking out the window.
"Wait a minute, Mavis!" he called out. "What have you got there?"
"Oh, just my fine worm," said Larky Mavis nervously, and hurried on.
The schoolmaster put on his hat and coat and followed after.

"Stop a minute, Mavis," called the doctor from his car. "What is that you have?"

"Oh, just my little bat," said Larky Mavis, and hurried even faster.

The doctor hopped from his car just as the schoolmaster was passing.

"Did you notice that child that Mavis has?" he asked. "Deformed, poor thing. I'm going to give it some treatments and write an article."

"What?" squealed the schoolmaster. "And ruin my specimen? I'm going to put it in my collection." The schoolmaster had a collection of things preserved in bottles which he called Natural History.

Larky Mavis heard them shouting behind her and began to run . . .

. . . smack into the parson!

"Oh, Father, they want to take away my fine little mouse," she cried.

"Your fine little mouse?" said the parson, peering closely. "Oh dear! How extraordinary! I think you'd better give him to me, Mavis." His voice was kind, but the hand that took her sleeve was quick.

Just then up rushed the schoolmaster and the doctor.
"Hold her!" they cried together, catching at her arms and collar.
"Now, Mavis, you must give it to me," pleaded the schoolmaster.
"It needs a doctor's care," cried the doctor.

Larky Mavis didn't know what to do. But just then a clear voice said:

LET GO MY MA!

Mavis hugged Heart's Delight close, and the doctor, the schoolmaster, the parson, and all the others fell back, as startled as if someone had rung the church bells in their ears.

I got to run, thought Mavis, but somehow her feet wouldn't carry her away. No, not at all. Instead, she was floating up in the air.

"Look!" she cried happily to Heart's Delight. "They look exactly like the mice and the moles!" And so they did, all the people running around beneath them.

Heart's Delight smiled and held her tight, and off they flew higher and higher.

Where did they go? Ah, nobody knows. Maybe it was just down the road or over the hill to a cottage by the sea. Or maybe, just maybe, it was far, far away, to another land altogether, where babies grow in peanut shells . . .

. . . and even worms have wings.